Ready, Set, OPA!

Demetra Tsavaris-Lecourezos
Co-creator Constantinos "Gus" Lecourezos

Illustrations by Marina Saumell

Published in the USA by *thewordverve inc.* (www.thewordverve.com)

eBook ISBN: 978-1-941251-95-9
Hardback ISBN: 978-1-941251-96-6

Library of Congress Control Number: 2017931650

Ready, Set, OPA!

A book with Verve by *thewordverve inc.*

Artwork by Marina Samuel
www.marimell.com

Book design by Robin Krauss
www.bookformatters.com

eBook formatting by Bob Houston
facebook.com/eBookFormatting

I dedicate this book to my late brother,
Constantine "Dean" Tsavaris,
a brilliant man and kind soul. Gone too soon.

"Dean-o Dream-o" . . . far too many of us weren't ready to live
a life without you . . . your kindness, thoughtfulness, numerous
phone calls, childlike smile and innocence.
We miss you so very much.

Young World Travelers

We're the Young World Travelers,
off again we go.
Our world is such an awesome place—
ready . . . set . . . let's go!

So much in our world to see,
whether in the air or on the sea.
To travel near or very far,
ride in a train or get in a car.

Each destination we seek,
has charm and is very unique.
Filled with beauty, history, and grace—
something to admire and embrace.

Tickets, passports and luggage in hand,
sail, fly, or drive to adventureland
Museums, architecture, sites, and tours—
a camera's a must for each visitor.

From a small island to a large city,
Trav'ling our world that's oh so pretty.
Country, Capital, Continent, Nation
Let's explore and visit this destination . . .

5

George, Eleni, and Maria bounced happily down the aisle of the jet plane that would soon take them to Greece. Their mom and dad followed closely behind, smiling at their children's excitement. It would be the children's first visit to Greece. Their adventures would begin once they arrived on the mainland in Athens.

"Daddy, this is a huge plane!" George exclaimed, doing a little dance as he headed toward his seat. "Wow! Did you see the pilot? I can't believe he let me wear his hat, and he gave me this toy plane! You said this was supposed to be such a long trip. What are we going to do for so many hours?" His words tumbled out, and he had to stop to take a deep breath.

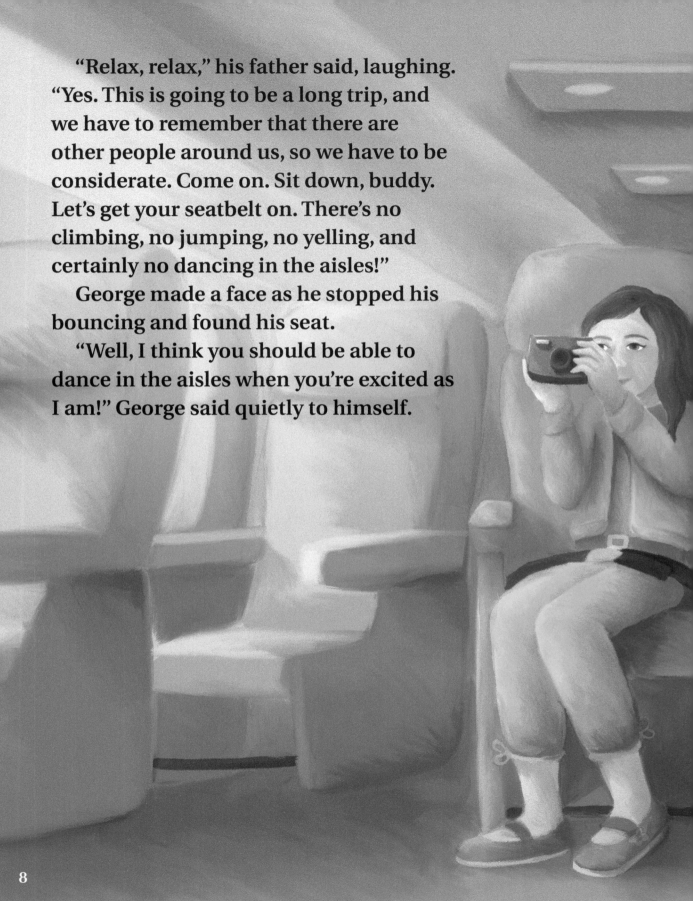

"Relax, relax," his father said, laughing. "Yes. This is going to be a long trip, and we have to remember that there are other people around us, so we have to be considerate. Come on. Sit down, buddy. Let's get your seatbelt on. There's no climbing, no jumping, no yelling, and certainly no dancing in the aisles!"

George made a face as he stopped his bouncing and found his seat.

"Well, I think you should be able to dance in the aisles when you're excited as I am!" George said quietly to himself.

Once in Athens, they plodded toward the Baggage Claim area, where they were shocked to see . . .

"Surprise!" shouted Stas, Leah, and Billy.

"Wow!" Maria's voice squeaked with excitement at seeing her cousins. "What are YOU all doing here?!"

"I wanted to see Mrs. Eva's Magical Crystal Globe in action," Stas said, laughing.

"We arrived last week. We came to visit with *Yiayia* and *Pappou* too," Leah added.

Eleni noticed something in Billy's hand. "What's that, Billy?"

"My bouzouki."

"It looks like a guitar to me," Eleni teased.

"*Yiasas, pedia*! These are for you," said *Yiayia*, handing Maria two dolls.

"What does that mean?" George asked.

"*Yiasas, pedia* means 'hello, kids,'" *Pappou* replied. He tousled George's hair playfully.

Maria grasped *Yiayia's* hand and said, "I love my dolls, *Yiayia*. Thank you!"

"They are *koukles* for my *koukla*! . . . Dolls for my doll," said *Yiayia*.

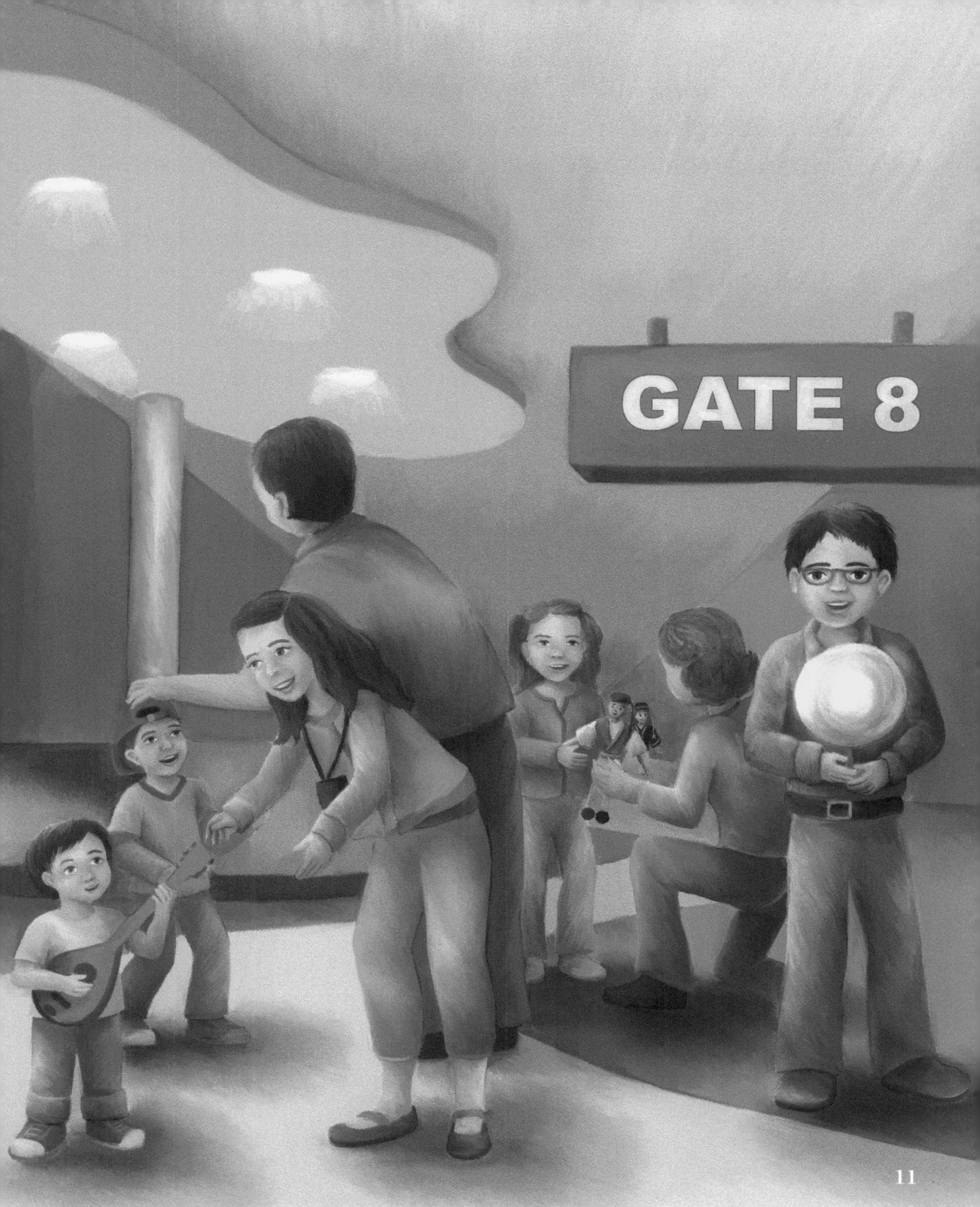
GATE 8

While waiting for their luggage, the kids passed the time with the Magical Crystal Globe, inputting the English spelling of words so that the globe could translate them into Greek.

Eleni said, "Let's try E-N-T-E-R."

The Magical Crystal Globe responded with: "*EE-SO-DOS.*"

Leah typed in L-U-G-G-A-G-E.

ΕΙΣΟΔΟΣ
ENTRANCE

The globe said: "*VA-LEE-TSES.*"

George reached for the globe and said, "My turn! Can I type a word, Eleni?"

Eleni held the Magical Crystal Globe as George typed W-E-L-C-O-M-E.

It replied: "*KA-LOS IR-THA-TE.*"

Maria jumped up and down excitedly. "That is SO cool! I have another one! How about 'Olympic Games'?"

ΒΑΛΙΤΣΕΣ
LUGGAGE

"Wait! I have an idea. Let's close our eyes,"
said Eleni, tugging on her mom's arm.

"And imagine," said George, nodding his
head as he held his dad's hand.

"Where will we go?" asked Stas.

14

"How about a festival where we can all pretend to be Greek gods and goddesses?" Dad suggested.
They all closed their eyes . . . and imagined.

Stas read the sign in front of them: "*Olympiako Stadio*, home of the Olympics. What's that?"

"*Olympiako Stadio* is how you say 'Olympic Stadium' in Greek," replied *Yiayia*.

Pappou said, "Let's pretend they are going to have the Olympic competitions just as they had them in ancient times. We can dress just like the gods did then, and we can compete to win a crown made of olive tree leaves and branches . . . and a medal, of course."

"What is that flag for?" asked Maria.

"All of the world competes in the Olympics, right? The five rings on that flag represent each of the five continents: Africa, the Americas, Asia, Europe, and Oceania," *Yiayia* explained. "At least one of those colors appears in the flag of each country that competes. This way, no one feels left out."

OLYMPIAKO
STADIO

17

"I am Zeus," said George, holding a thunderbolt. "King of gods and men. And king of thunder and lightning. I gather clouds and send rain."

"I am Athena. Goddess of wisdom," Eleni said. "I have no mother. I sprang full grown and dressed in this armor from the forehead of my father, Zeus."

Stas walked out from behind the curtain, holding a trident. "I am the brother of Zeus. God of the sea, anger, and earthquakes. I live in a palace of gold, deep in the Aegean Sea and am Athena's uncle. Can you guess who I am?" He waited. No one responded, so he said in a deep voice, "I am Poseidon."

Maria held a wreath high in the air. "I am Nike, the winged goddess of victory. I float in the air with spread wings, pointing to a new victor."

"And I am Aphrodite," said Leah. "Goddess of love and beauty. Wherever I walk, flowers grow and doves follow me."

Billy shouted, "I'm Hercules! I can lift this water bottle!"

Pappou explained, "Many of the sports we enjoy today didn't exist in ancient times. Some of the big events were held at Mount Olympia. They included wrestling, jumping, discus throwing, boxing, and horseracing. The games were so important that all people's differences were forgotten during the time of the Olympics—even wars ceased. And all were united during that time, even if only temporarily."

"What about running, or marathons?" Eleni asked.

"Running, yes. But marathons didn't come until many years later. Actually, Marathon is a place. And when the Athenians won the war against the Persians, a Greek soldier with bleeding feet ran all the way from Marathon to Athens to announce their big victory. It was about a 25-mile distance filled with obstacles and hills. That's where the word 'marathon' comes from. The true distance for a marathon is 26.2 miles."

Leah asked "What about triathlons?"

"They weren't included in the Olympics until 1920. In Greek, *tria* means three—"

"Like in tricycle!" Stas exclaimed.

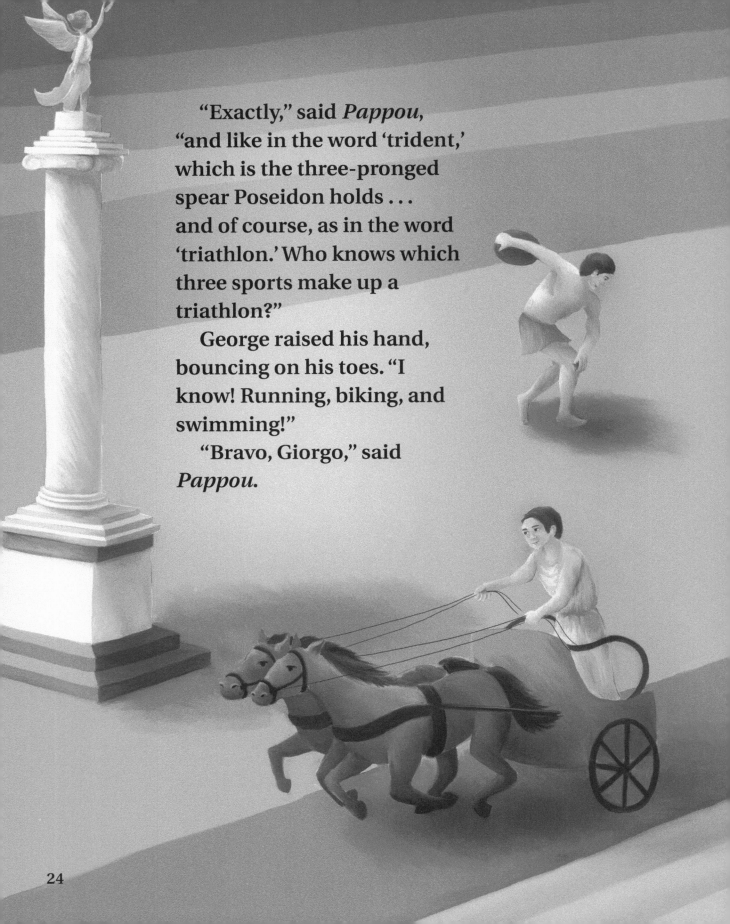

"Exactly," said *Pappou*, "and like in the word 'trident,' which is the three-pronged spear Poseidon holds . . . and of course, as in the word 'triathlon.' Who knows which three sports make up a triathlon?"

George raised his hand, bouncing on his toes. "I know! Running, biking, and swimming!"

"Bravo, Giorgo," said *Pappou.*

The next morning, everyone got together in the hotel lobby to meet their guide for a tour of the Acropolis.

Suddenly, Dad said, "*Kali mera, Kiria* Eva, and Katerina!

The children's heads whipped around as they searched for the familiar faces of Mrs. Eva and Katerina. When they saw them, they screamed excitedly and ran to them for hugs.

"SURPRISE! *Yiasas*, everyone," said Mrs. Eva, "and *kalos irthate* to *Ellada!*"

"I know you just said 'welcome to Greece.' We've been using our Magical Crystal Globe, *Kiria* Eva. This really is a surprise," said Maria, holding her hand on her chest, her heart thumping wildly.

"I'm glad to hear that, Maria." Mrs. Eva clapped her hands and said to the group, "Well, if we're all ready, let's get going. We have many adventures to tackle today!"

"Look up, everyone," said Mrs. Eva. "That is the Acropolis. Isn't it just beautiful? Does anyone know what acropolis means?"

Eleni raised her hand quickly. "I do! I do! It means 'high city.'"

"Bravo, Eleni," Mrs. Eva said. "On the Acropolis, there are many buildings which make up the city. At the highest point is the Parthenon. It is all marble, and it took about nine years to build. See the point, or the triangle, at the top? That is called the pediment. And the flat part that wraps around the top is called the frieze. As we walk around the Parthenon, look carefully at the detail on the frieze. It tells many stories about Greek history and wars, the gods and mythology, and the Olympic Games."

Mrs. Eva continued, "In ancient times, the pediment and the frieze were in bright, beautiful colors. There are very few images today which show the colors anymore."

She lifted the Magical Crystal Globe in the air and said, "Let's imagine what that looked like."

The children closed their eyes and could see the Parthenon as it once was.

"Oooh, ahhh," they exclaimed.

Stas pointed to the top of the Parthenon and asked, "Excuse me, *Kiria* Eva, can you tell us what those are?"

"Those are called centaurs. In mythological stories, they are creatures who are part man and part horse."

"Wow! They're scary looking!"

"Come," said Mrs. Eva, guiding them around the side of the Parthenon. "Thousands of years of wars, earthquakes, acid rain, and pollution in the air have destroyed so much of this beautiful place." She pointed to the structure. "There are fifteen columns on each side, and eight columns on the front and on the back. It is 101 feet by 228 feet . . . not quite the size of a football field, but pretty close."

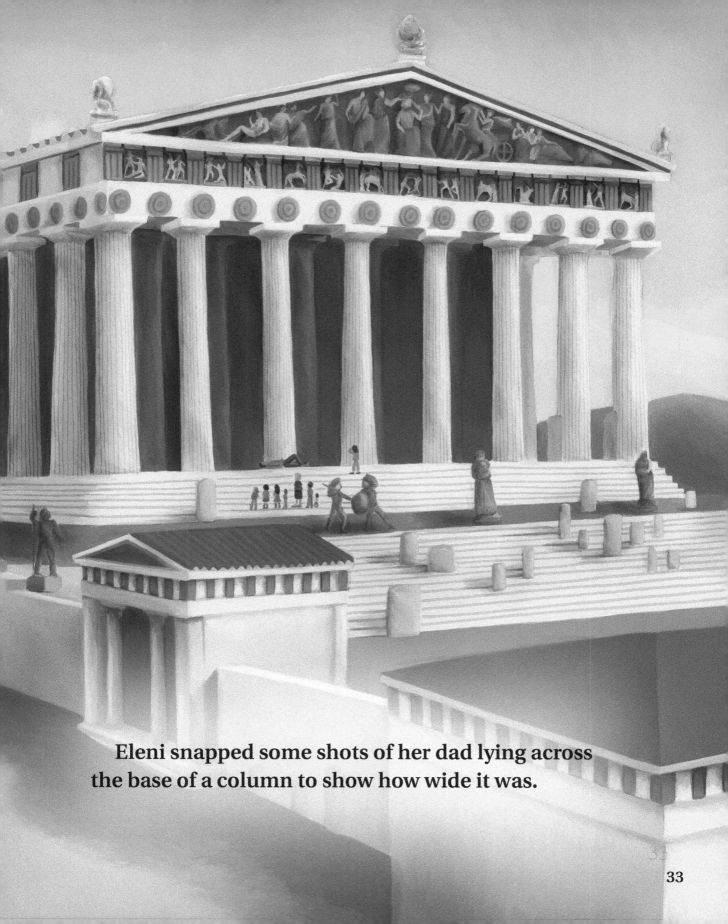

Eleni snapped some shots of her dad lying across
the base of a column to show how wide it was.

"Who is THAT?" asked George as they approached a huge statue.

Mrs. Eva said, "The Parthenon was built in honor of the Patroness Athena. They created this statue of her, made of wood and covered in gold and ivory. She wears a helmet on her head, holds a Nike statue in her hand, which symbolizes victory, and a spear at her side. Next to her feet, near the spear, is a snake. The snake is said to help Athena protect the city. To give you an idea of how big she is, just the base alone is five feet tall. See? We're looking at her toes!"

Billy scrambled to sit on his father's shoulders and wrinkled his nose at the toes of the great statue.

"Oh! And next to the Parthenon, over this way . . . this is my favorite. This porch is called Caryatids. Instead of the typical columns, these girls are holding up the roof of this porch. See? The girls are said to have come from an ancient city called Caryes. Real maids probably modeled for this."

"Why would they have cleaning women model for this?" Leah asked.

Mrs. Eva laughed. "When we say maids, Leah, we mean young girls of beauty, purity, and femininity."

Eleni started snapping pictures of the beautiful ladies. George, Stas and Billy kept sticking their heads in the pictures, laughing hysterically.

"In the early 1800s," Mrs. Eva said, "a British lord, Lord Elgin, removed much of the frieze of the Parthenon and one of these ladies. They were sent to the British Museum via ship. While some of those ships sank, there are still a lot of what are known as the Elgin Marbles from the Acropolis in the British Museum. To preserve the remaining five maids, they were removed from here and put in the Acropolis Museum. What you are now looking at are replicas, all made of plaster."

Mrs. Eva looked up at the maids and sighed. "Legend tells us that when the first maiden was stolen, the others wept at night for their departed sister."

"Wow," said Katerina, clasping her hands together. "They look like they have been here forever, as if they are the originals! They're so beautiful!"

"Have we enjoyed our day?" Mrs. Eva asked. A beautiful sunset filled the sky behind her.

An enthusiastic chorus of "Yes!" came from the group.

"I learned so much. I feel like my brain is full," said Katerina.

Mrs. Eva chuckled. "You must all be tired, but we'll get to relax now. We're now at a place called Microlimano, which means 'small port.' Does 'micro,' also pronounced 'mee-kro,' sound familiar to any of you?"

Stas thought for a moment. "Like in microscope?"

"Exactly! Bravo, Stas," Mrs. Eva replied. "At Microlimano, there are many *tavernas*, or what we would call restaurants, overlooking the water and colorful fishing boats. We will listen to bouzouki music as we eat, and we will see some dancers perform in traditional Greek costumes."

"Opa!" said Katerina, and the others joined in the celebratory cheer.

MOUSSAKA

PASTITSIO

HORIATIKI
SALATA

BAKLAVA

At a big table overlooking the water, the family enjoyed a grand feast of Greek cuisine. They'd decided to order a variety of foods, so that everyone could try a little of everything.

Their waiter, Kostas, was never far from them, making sure the group had everything they needed.

When the meal was complete, *Pappou* asked Kostas for the check.

"I think we've eaten just about all we can. *Efharisto*, Kostas, for all your help serving this wonderful meal."

"*Parakalo*," Kostas replied.

"*Efharisto* means 'thank you' and *parakalo* means 'you're welcome,'" Stas said. "Right, *Pappou*?"

Pappou beamed with pride. "Very good, Stas."

Once their bellies were full and they could barely keep their eyes open, the group headed back to the hotel for a good night's rest. Tomorrow would take them to Sparta.

After a hearty breakfast, the group headed out for their next adventure. Dad was excited to show them one particular piece of history in the city of Sparta. When they got there, he pointed and said, "This is a monument of one of the country's greatest heroes, King Leonidas of Sparta."

"Leonidas means 'lion-like,'" *Yiayia* added.

"I recognize him by the Greek letter lambda on his shield," Leah said. "I saw a picture in one of our tourist brochures."

Stas adjusted the warrior helmet his Dad had purchased for him at one of the souvenir shops. "Why was he a hero?"

"Leonidas was the king that led the 300 Spartans into battle at Thermopylae," said *Pappou*. "He was one of the greatest military leaders in Greek history. In ancient times, boys younger than you were sent away from home to military training, and would become soldiers when they turned twenty."

ΜΟΛΩΝ ΛΑΒΕ

ΤΟΝΔΕ ΑΝΔΡΙΑΝΤΑ
ΒΑΣΙΛΕΩΣ ΛΕΩΝΙΔΑ
ΣΥΝ ΤΩ ΗΡΩΩ ΤΟΥΤΩ
Ο ΕΚ ΛΑΚΕΔΑΙΜΟΝΟΣ
ΠΑΝΟΣ Σ. ΚΟΥΜΑΝΤΑΡΟΣ
ΤΗ ΣΠΑΡΤΗ ΑΝΕΘΗΚΕΝ
1968

"Wow! I can't imagine leaving home for so many years," Stas said.

"See the writing on the base there?" Dad said. "It reads *Molon Lave*, which translates to 'Come and get them.' That was Leonidas' response when the enemy's emperor demanded that the Spartans surrender their weapons."

Billy and George made muscles and puffed out their chests.

"We're the mighty Spartans," George said.

As the laughter at their antics died down, Mrs. Eva said, "Children, it has been delightful to explore with you again. As much as we have learned about Greece here on the mainland, there are still so many more things to discover about her glorious islands across the Aegean Sea."

"We can always look forward to adventures with the help of our Magical Crystal Globe, Mrs. Eva. I can't wait for all the fun we will have when we take it to Egypt for my birthday!" said Katerina.

Mrs. Eva smiled and added, "Remember to share your travel experiences with your friends and family. Write down your thoughts, take pictures, let your mind absorb all the stories you hear. After all, imagination and understanding are sparked by the lessons we share."

"We are the young world travelers!" said Katerina. She lifted her fist in the air, and the others did the same.

Mt. Olympus

GREECE

Aegean Sea

Athens

Marathon

Pireus

Sparta

Mediterranean Sea

Destination Examination Questions

1. What sports make up a triathlon?

2. What do the five rings on the Olympic flag represent?

3. What do the colors on the Olympic flag represent?

4. King Leonidas and the 300 warriors are from which city?

5. Name one thing that tells us stories about life in mythological times.

6. Who is the "Goddess of Victory"?

7. Mythological monsters are called what?

8. What is the distance in a marathon?

9. Name a Greek musical instrument.

10. Who was the Parthenon built in honor of?

Demetra Tsavaris-Lecourezos, Author

Born and raised in Queens, NY, Demetra has spent over a decade planning her educational series of children's books intended to be a "reference library" of travel from a child's perspective. The idea was born shortly after her daughter Katerina was welcomed into the world; Demetra and her late husband, Constantinos "Gus" Lecourezos, wanted to create a fun and educational format for kids to learn about the world: EDU-TAINMENT!

Unfortunately, Gus would not live to see the dream come to fruition—he died of pancreatic cancer when Katerina was just four years old. Life changed dramatically for Demetra and her daughter, and the two ultimately moved to Tapon Springs, FL, where Demetra continued her career in interior and event design.

In 2013, she decided to revive the dream that she and Gus had started—the first book, *Young World Travelers and the Magical Crystal Globe* was published in 2014. The book was immediately embraced by readers, including a five-star rating from the respected Reader's Favorite program.

Shortly after the book's publication, cancer hit home again. Demetra is now fighting her own battle with cancer.

With a survivor attitude already deeply ingrained inside her, she took only a brief respite before forging into the second book, *Ready, Set, OPA!* Throughout her cancer treatment, she has actively participated in its creation, as has her spirited daughter, Katerina.

Demetra is a member of the Society of Children's Book Writers and Illustrators.

Demetra is available for book signings, storytelling and author talks. She has presented at schools, libraries, camps, fundraisers and other similar events. To request an author appearance, please email **ywtbooks@gmail.com.**

Marina Saumell, Illustrator

Marina Saumell resides in Mar del Plata, Argentina, with her husband and two children. She has a degree in architecture and worked as an architect for several years.

Her love for children's books inspired her to become a freelance illustrator following the birth of her first child.

"EDU-TAINMENT"

Ready, Set, Opa! is the second book in a series about a group of children who travel the world along with their Magical Crystal Globe. Taking the reader on many exciting journeys, it is intended to be a "reference library" of travel from a child's perspective. From story to story, the young world travelers share the histories of each place they visit, the cultures, the architecture, the modes of travel, currency, food and music, to name a few. The series also incorporates the concepts of sharing and manners, compassion and empathy, and integrity.

The first book, *Young World Travelers and the Magical Crystal Globe,* kicks off the adventures from Tarpon Springs, Florida, to Queens, New York.

The educational aspect along with the uplifting camaraderie combine to offer a new form of learning: *edu-tainment!*